D0680621

Creative Director: Susie Garland Rice
Art Director: Dan Waters

Dalmatian Press owns all art and editorial material.
ISBN: 1-57759-274-3
© 1999 Dalmatian Press. All rights reserved.
Printed and bound in the U.S.A. The DALMATIAN PRESS name,
logo and spotted spine are trademarks of Dalmatian Press, Franklin, Tennessee 37067.
Written permission must be secured from the publisher to use or reproduce any part of this book.

10752a/boywhocriedwolf

The **Boy** who **Cried Wolf**

An ÆSOP Fable
adapted by **Martha Stamps**
illustrated by **Jeff Fuqua**

Dalmatian Press

Once there was a little shepherd boy with a big job. Every day he looked after his father's sheep as they grazed in the hills.

Although it wasn't difficult, his job was still important. There were wolves who lived in the hills, and their favorite meal was plump and juicy sheep. If he ever saw a wolf, the boy's special job was to blow his horn and cry, "Wolf! Wolf! Wolf!" Then his father and brothers would run up the hill and scare away the wolf.

The shepherd boy had been lucky and had never seen a wolf, but he didn't think he was so lucky. He grew bored watching the sheep. He wanted some excitement.

One day, as the sheep were peacefully grazing, the shepherd boy blew on his horn and cried, "Wolf! Wolf! Wolf!"

He laughed when he saw his father and brothers running up the hill as fast as they could. "Where is the wolf?" they demanded to know, panting from the hard run. "I must have made a mistake," the little boy fibbed. "Perhaps I saw a rabbit running into the woods."

His father and brothers were glad that the shepherd and sheep were safe. His father said, "Son, it's very difficult for us to run all the way up here. Be sure that there really is trouble before you call for help." Then the men returned to their jobs.

"That was fun!" the boy thought. "They looked silly running up the hill!" He decided that as soon as the men got down the hill, he would play the same trick again. He blew his horn and cried, "Wolf! Wolf! Wolf!" His father and brothers ran up the hill as fast as they could.

There was no wolf, and his brothers were angry. They didn't like being tricked. His father asked, "Do you know what happens to boys who make up stories and play tricks? Soon nobody believes anything they say."

"But it's not a story," the boy fibbed.

He laughed as the men went back down the hill. "Aren't I clever? I fooled them all!" He was so pleased with himself that he tried the trick again!

This time his brothers didn't want to run up the hill, but their father said, " He might be in trouble! We have to go!" His father was sad to find that his boy had lied again. He could no longer trust his son.

The boy was still laughing when suddenly he heard the bleating of a lamb. He looked up just in time to see a wolf dragging the lamb into the woods. The shepherd blew on his horn and cried, "Wolf! Wolf! Wolf!" but no one came running. Even the boy's father didn't believe him this time. All the shepherd boy could do was hide behind a tree as the wolf stole all of the sheep.

When night time fell, the boy sadly made his way down the hill to his father, who cried, "Son, where are our sheep?"

"Didn't you hear me calling?" the pitiful shepherd asked. "There really was a wolf, and now he's eaten up all of our sheep!"

"We heard, but how could we believe you when you had lied to us before?"

"Oh father," cried the boy, "I did a terrible thing. Can you ever forgive me?"

"I will always forgive you, son. Losing our sheep is a stiff price to pay, but if you have learned the danger of playing pranks and telling lies, this is a lesson well learned." The boy kissed his father and solemnly promised to always tell the truth. Never again did the boy tell a lie, and he became the very best shepherd in the entire land.

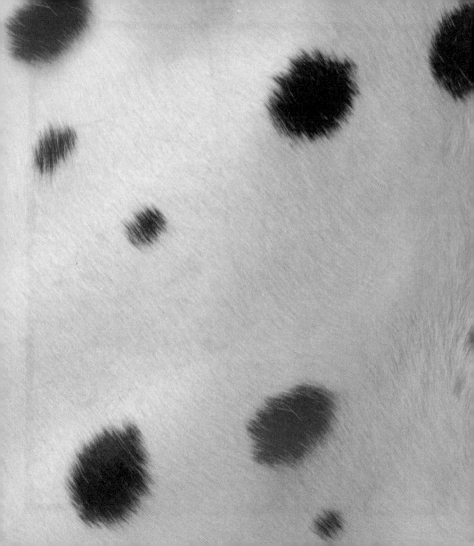